Aleatory on the Radio

Also by Angela Carole Brown

Trading Fours, 2005

The Assassination of Gabriel Champion, 2013

The Kidney Journals: Memoirs of a Desperate Lifesaver, 2014

Bones, 2019

Viscera, 2019

Aleatory on the Radio

& other 100-Word Stories

Angela Carole Brown

H A I K U   H O U S E

Aleatory on the Radio

Cover photo of the Penn State Millennium Science Complex and graphic layout
by Angela Carole Brown
Author photo by Sandy Brooke

Visit Angela's website at: www.angelacarolebrown.com
Purchase her books at: www.bit.ly/BooksByAngelaCaroleBrown

Published by Haiku House
First Edition
ISBN-13: 978-1-7337453-1-4

In Hamlet, the character of Polonius describes brevity as *"...the soul of wit, And tediousness the limbs and outward flourishes..."* Shakespeare is being humorous here, as Polonius actually rambles on and on, in making his point. Nevertheless, point made. Stumbling quite by accident upon the 100-word-story world, I became enthralled by this form as I read some electrifying miniatures, also variously known as flash fiction, postcard fiction, microfiction, drabbles, short-shorts, and bite-sized fiction. There are some definite masters at this. And I was gripped by this idea of something so taut it rattles the usual instincts. Imagine scrutinizing each word and, most especially, wrenching meaning from the spaces between (as what is un-said is as critical as what is said). That the breadth of tragedy or celebration within the self-control of strictly counted words can be *infinite* moved me to act, to explore, to see for myself what I might be capable of. Ernest Hemingway used the iceberg as a metaphor for writing—to reveal only the top 10% of your story, leaving the other 90% below water to be imagined. That has been an exciting lesson that I have spent the past two years trying my best to hone, as I proceeded to write toward my own collection. *Aleatory on the Radio* offers tiny odysseys that turn their own worlds inside out. They illustrate the ironic nature of perspective, and that we never truly know the whole story. Weaving through the vista of artists, loners, lovers, losers, dreamers, those lost, those found, this collection of microstories explores a world as baffling as it is beautiful.

Contents

Aleatory on the Radio
& other 100-Word Stories

stories   refracted light at oblique angles

After the Thousandth Time Singing Lush Life

This couple isn't married. He has a wife at home. That guy's getting dumped. Check out her pity face. Even I know she's about to lower the boom. This couple in the corner? You can practically see the pheromones leaping off the red leather booth, skank dust. Strayhorn's "Lush Life" is heartbreak and anesthesia. I tend to open a vein when singing her, but tonight I just want the wound to stay sealed, so I let the audience distract me. Look at that girl too young to be in here, trying to nurse her own wounds. All these come-what-may faces.

Nighted Color

He shared his weed. They swapped some fluids. My place or yours? The front seat sufficed. "My father just died," he suddenly said. Such startling intimacies he would share with her, a stranger, and he cried on her dashboard. She wanted to cradle him, but thought better of it. There's a reason you don't exchange names; keeps the wall up, necessary in this game. When she got home, she Febrezed the car, went inside, sat, and felt her unexpected heart swiftly ache for the nameless, fatherless child who was surely out there still, burying his pain between some other legs.

Ruby Red

William always found Beth's habit of writing little love notes on the bathroom mirror with her lipstick irresistible. How utterly infectious the young. He was a good twenty years her senior, and she had breathed life back into him after his divorce. But the lipstick on the mirror—that was the sealant. He adored her unpredictability. When he came home one night to find his house empty of everything, including Beth, William's heart pounded until the numbness set in. Snapping to, he ran to the bathroom to see if she had, at least, honored him with a ruby red goodbye.

The Lifespan of Gardens

Corrugated drums sprout from cement along the banks of the L.A. River, graffiti-graced. The L.A. River ISN'T ...exactly. It funnels an urban run-off down a concrete gully. Once the source of L.A.'s freshwater, a task replaced by aqueducts, today it serves punchlines more than civic duty. Ma'am, you'll no longer need yearly pap smears. She's always hated paps, yet is surprised by grief. *Your cervix is a raisin*, is what she hears. She thinks about the run-off, barely useful anymore except as fodder for sad L.A. stories. Like the river, however inert, she just continues flowing, gathering stories like silt.

Supernova

He sold the painted canvas on the street for $1, a striking abstract created by his own homeless hands. Years later it sold at a gallery for $800. The original purchaser, an artist himself, had put his own name on it. By the time many more years passed, and it sold at Sotheby's for a million (as the artist/thief eventually enjoyed astronomical fame), the homeless man, who never thought of his painting again beyond that corner sell, had long ago died, impoverished. The art thief did not fear God. He did, however, feel the dread of ghosts now and again.

Splenic Descent

They had their biggest and final fight in the middle of the Lucian Freud exhibit, a collection of works that could awaken the starkest fears of alienation. Maggie had been wondrously transported by the visceral nature of Freud's putrescent nudes, actually weeping to be so shattered. Even as Jasper was utterly repulsed by the portraits that surrounded them, nearly spitting at what he found ugly. She hated that he couldn't see the potent layers of beauty beneath the torpid, decaying flesh. And he hated her hypocrite's pretentiousness in the rude face of her own disgust whenever he undressed for her.

Alms

She is something to see with the homeless. Me, I've always called myself compassionate, especially regarding the disenfranchised. But she will follow her own offering of whatever's in her pocket with, *"what's your story?"* And here's the remarkable rub—she truly wants to sit and find out. Not judge. Not preach. Simply listen. "The only thing anyone truly wants in this life is to be heard." I marvel at her grace. The best I have in me is to give them my dollar and run away as quickly as possible, fear fevering from me like so many beads of sweat.

Ghosts & Guile

He tried selling his bogus Dallas Morning News copies of that fateful day in 1963 by claiming to've been in the crowd when Kennedy was shot, even though he was years away from being born. He hawked his wares every morning at Dealey Plaza, longing for connection to legend, the trophy of proximity. *"His blood actually sprayed on me!"* The blood of purpose, where his own seemed to hold none. After enough times recited, story became conviction. The brain is funny that way. It can just as vulnerably explode upon bullet impact as it can powerfully twist fiction into truth.

While Gaily Leafing

She gaily leafed through old dogeared notebooks to reminisce on what she had journaled over the years. The early ones had entire novels in them, brazen adventures, horizons rudely breached, flight. Gradually her scribbles flowered into a mesmerizing self-help fog. Magical-thinking platitudes. Affirmations that, ironically, only affirmed the "I'm not good enough as I am" story. And lists (oh, the lists!) of all the things she planned on manifesting. Because... well... things. From the vast realm of boundlessness to the vaguely panicked mindset of lack she soared over valleys, like a California Adventure attraction holding on way too white-knuckle tight.

Duet

I see you sitting there struggling. Wondering what right thing to say to me because I can no longer speak. But though I can't—I see you. I do. When you touch my hand I feel it, and I know that love is the reason you've come. We both know I'm not here much longer, so why bother with politeness? Curse at me for dying. Tell a stupid joke. Or better yet, sing. Remember that song? The one I'd always request of you? Oh, sing that one. I'll throw a harmony on top. But you won't know that, will you?

The Art Piece

He completely gets the Dharmic lesson of neither indulging nor resisting pain but instead simply flowing with and honoring the experience until it passes, which this too shall. But for the life of him, he can't identify the compassion in neglecting to plug into even a moment of commiseration. How much he would've appreciated getting a simple "I'm so sorry" from his friend the abbot, whom he kind of worships, upon exclaiming that the art piece they're staring at reminds him of his recently departed father. The breezeless monastic demeanor suddenly piques even more of his fascination than the painting.

The Monastery

She walked up, her turn to bestow a blessing on the monks. This part of the ceremony marked the layman's chance to give back. She tried to hear what those before her were saying. She knew that something sage would be expected, and she doubted her skill for this hallowed task. When she offered to the first monk some underwhelming, rote mumblings about peace, and inspired in him a fit of the chuckles, all her romanticism about unflappable monastic life was dashed. He'd shown her the ordinary dude that lurked beneath those lofty saffron robes. He also had her number.

Nail Heads

She laid everything out on tarps and blankets, covering the front lawn that was wet from the morning fog, but she knew that would burn off with the first sun. It was time to let go of his things. Time to let go of pain, and war, and memory. As she nailed a giant, handwritten sign that read "everything must go" to a telephone pole, she was queerly drawn to the hundreds of rusted nail heads still embedded in the pole's cylindrical wood, from a hundred other garage sales, a hundred other stories, a hundred other rituals for letting go.

The Disquieting

Their most favorite boyhood pastime was hiding from the two men. The two men were trench-coated boogeymen with no faces except the shadows cast by their fedoras, like in *The Third Man*. The two men were wholly conjured by the brothers' wild imaginations. They loved the rush of being chased, even if imaginary, with the thicket of their backyard serving as the dark alley. When, years later, two men actually did attack his brother, a random home invasion that took his brother and his brother's wife and kid, he spent the rest of his life waiting, hexed, for his turn.

Laura

Many nights she perched against the wall of Ralphs. She never slept in a bed, but on the floor of her living room. All signs pointed to her having once been homeless. She wasn't now; she lived in my building. I often drove her on errands. Invariably after such, I'd find a scented candle on my doorstep. Laura was kind. It broke my heart the day she threatened suicide and wouldn't let the paramedics in. I had run downstairs and opened the gate for them. But instead of feeling like I'd helped, I felt the very traitor she called me.

Threnody for Coitus and Piano

Each time she let him inside, she had to release him afterwards by sitting to the Steinway. For lovemaking that bordered on a tempest, Beethoven's Sonata Pathétique worked its magic. Whenever he touched her with tenderness, it was usually a Chopin Nocturne that unloosed him. Bartok Bagatelles tended to work best following the kinkier proclivities, the ones he loved but she tolerated. Today, as she prepared to wrestle the foreboding, impetuous Rachmaninoff Prelude in C$\sharp$ minor, she wondered if it could even remotely do justice to her loss, her abject sorrow that she had ever needed to routinely release him.

The Waiting Room

It seemed the waiting would never end. He paced, while obsessing over the flood of texts between him and his wife that grew increasingly explosive. His phone beeped nonstop. He tried to restructure his last response, tried to tap the screen to edit, forgetting for just an instant that there are no retractions in a text; his confession would be forever stamped in her brain. One more plea. Nicer this time. She's the one devastated, after all. His thumbs started their furious dance. This wait might just kill him. "Mr. Jones, would you like to see your new baby girl?"

Intersection

In the days of rain, verdant fields moved like lovers. Spring seared bonds and spun burlap into silk. She loved only him, for he looked past the ropes of flesh bound and braided, creating hills around loose skin and vigilance. He'd undressed first. Tattoos galore. But beyond that, scarifications. Some kind of tribal thing from his travels? Made her feel much better about the radical mastectomy chest she was sporting, and the decision against reconstruction. It had been a statement, perhaps also tribal, but then she'd found herself insecure. Now they were a tribe unto themselves. And each other loved.

In the Name of Love

She couldn't believe how much she missed getting so swept up in an incredible evening with a guy that it parlayed into intimacy, and spending the night, and sneaking out of his place in the morning to find the ticket on her windshield, and knowing full well, even in the throes of their lust, that 6am to 8am on Tuesdays was "no parking for street sweeping," and not caring one fig. She couldn't believe how much she missed the knots in her gut upon discovery, the wantonness of amassing a dauntless traffic violations record all in the name of love.

Two Stories

As he drove, they were having the most awful breakup fight he'd
ever experienced. In a moment of demolished despair, he slammed
his hands against the steering wheel, accidentally causing the car
horn to stick. He pulled over and thrust open the hood, trying
frantically to stop it, as his girlfriend sat numb amid the spirit-
crushing blare. A grieving family buries their patriarch. Ninety-
eight years of life and legacy. Family man. War hero. His children
have organized a stirring farewell and are now mortified to have
his graveside eulogy ruined by some road-rager somewhere
obnoxiously laying on his car horn.

A Special Attraction Comes to Town

We each get to meet our selves. As I encounter you, you are floating, submerged, behind the aquarium glass. Your face reflects a resolve I've never seen before. Child eyes catch mine, and I struggle to keep them locked. You think suffering will be assuaged by drowning. You think there is no peace but this. I am the manifest you, all the way from adulthood to assure you that you/we do come into our own. We become grace. Please kick your feet. Soar upwards. Retake in that huge gulp of life. We need look back—*only*—to witness the shift.

The Moment I Learned Lyle Waggoner Was Cool

We sweltered in the Arkansas humidity, as the house band rehearsed the celebrities who were slated to perform at the banquet. Later I'd get to take a picture with the governor. And who had any clue he was about to give us a decade of juicy scandals and a presidency? But that's neither here nor there. When Lyle Waggoner, my mother's era's heartthrob from *The Carol Burnett Show*, walked into rehearsal and told us to just play some blues, then proceeded to coolly style Tom Waits' "Frank's Wild Years," that damned Ken Doll had my undying worship from then on.

The Harrow

You keep waiting for an earthquake that'll shake loose this dust from the corners, and rattle the panes and the pains, or a harrow to gust up the creaks. You keep waiting for a diagnosis of cancer that'll finally frighten off the propensity to indulge in cancer-causing activities. You keep waiting for a venomous snakebite. A forcing to get still, make the plan for a radical rejuvenation. A furious overhaul of everything through an unsettling portal. Violence as cleansing: A *ripping* away of baggage, a *breaking* of patterns, a *demolition* of ideas past. Because the gentler schemes just haven't worked.

Scoliosis

The boyfriend asked if he could store his gun under her pillow. Though she was vehemently opposed to guns, she said yes. When she and her roommate decided to participate in the Women's March, she was afraid to tell him and ended up bailing on the historical event. He was the son of a jingoistic blowhard. But while his father and older brother wore their flag-waving swagger with relish, he was young and impressionable still, and looking for any excuse to defy Dad and be inspired elseways. But for a girlfriend who wielded little agency, and instead asked "how high?"

Let Me Fill Your Heart With Joy and Laughter

Today, at my first-ever goat yoga class, we were warned of the possibility that the baby goats might just relieve themselves. We were also promised it wouldn't be some mushy smelly affair, but more like an unoffending shower of dry pebbles. When one of the babies jumped up on my back as I did cat-cow, and proceeded to do his business, the first example yet, and on ME of all the people there, not only did the class applaud, but for just one moment I rode the coattails of this little starlet, sharing all of his scatological glory with him.

Sign Language

The click of electronic door locks from each car that stopped at the light stabbed just a little. Holding his sign and a threadbare knapsack, he never looked drivers in the eye from his perch at the freeway off-ramp. His presence, alone, without his pleas, would either move them or repel them. And while he couldn't really hear the clicks, he knew the move. Hand to the door. It was automatic. He'd been on the other side, himself, upon a time, so the fear was quite familiar. Today he was the one who instilled it. His hunger made him dangerous.

Immeasurable

Mae walked up to Coretta Scott King, a visiting speaker at her church, and with a tremble in her 8-year-old voice asked for Mrs. King's autograph on her Sunday program. When the widow of the most iconic man in the world politely declined, Mae walked away with that tremble taking up residence in her chin. Mere weeks before, Mrs. King had lost her husband, the apotheosis of the Civil Rights Movement. The woman's pain was immeasurable. An entire nation had erupted. Mae would never again think of Mrs. King without reliving the shun. An 8-year-old's pain can be immeasurable too.

Into the Gap

Being a rock star, he was consumed by music. Instead of it being a sacred portal, however, it started to serve as a barricade from silence. He used music as a drowning, to blunt the senses. Yet those senses were meant to be heightened and mined if he stood a chance in hell at being an artist. Easy to get crushed under the weight and clumsy thud of a sound-&-fury world. It's when he was able to move into the formless gap between thoughts that the undetectable realms could be cracked. Boundlessness restored. And the true rock star could emerge.

Orare

My mother had always dreamt of us visiting the Poets' Corner at Westminster Abbey together someday, and I ended up making that trip with someone else. I stood at the bones of Chaucer, Tennyson, Longfellow (his cherished book she'd given me), all the while silently begging her forgiveness that I'd treated her like old married couples sick of each other's breathing. How had we gotten here, mother and daughter, when she had been my world for a thousand years? I would never graduate from the heartbreak of standing before Samuel Taylor Coleridge without her hand to clutch, our girlish swoons.

Cachet

Howard and Miguel tied the knot the day it was made legal. They'd successfully lived the life of a married couple for decades, and finally they really were. It wasn't long before the pressures of the legality began to dig into their ribs, and before you could blink, a twenty-five-year relationship was shattering. They had overcome hate crimes, family abandonment, even an affair. What they had no notion of, until it was upon them, was that the signing of that piece of paper could kill a good thing quicker than the plague. It seemed like the cruelest hetero prank, frankly.

Bedazzled

Her involvement with the Panthers had always held romance for the child me, especially the steely resolve with which she entered such exotic terrain, even if notions of automatic-weapon-wielding agitators in black berets and fists in badass salute terrified me. She was passionate about revolution. I was just a child, no calling yet assigned. An abstract for me, frankly, I simply knew that I could never aspire to her clear, unfettered call to act. I deified Big Sis from my grubby-faced child's distance. But even more importantly, her massive Afro was so magnificent that I could barely breathe for swooning.

The Mediterranean at the End of the Block

At the end of the block lay the Mediterranean Sea. She walked the length of the cobbled street from her dilapidated bungalow toward its magnificence, stood on the warm shore, and gazed out at the tangerine horizon. As the swarthy gentleman approached and inquired if she found it mesmerizing that the other end of her stare held Africa's shore, she smiled and got the feeling this was his standard come-on. She was finally waking up after a coma of widowhood, and she considered this stranger. And she considered the sea. Each calling. Each nudging. Each with an offer of baptism.

An Unexpected Stance

On the whole, she prefers the nighttime. The moon. The stars. Intuition. Dreams. She loves the female energy of the dark. It seduces her much more powerfully than the cock-strutting day. Symbolically and poetically, in particular, she is drawn to the archetypal shadows of Jungian unconscious. The place where truth dwells. She finds beauty in the irony that examining the dark becomes a portal to the light, because uncovering always unburdens. Uncovering unburdens. #uncoveringunburdens. *Hmmm.* Interesting, how in creating a hashtag (her tiresome modern compulsion), the eye instinctively sees "gun burdens." It wasn't her point. But hell, she'll take it.

A Major Arcanum

He drew the Tower card in a playful Tarot reading at a friend's party and instantly knew that his tribe was about to abandon him; the card merely confirmed what he'd already sensed. They no longer understood him. They rejected his spiritual path, threatened him with Hell. His rebirth would leave him alienated. He had to determine which he treasured more, his enlightenment or his people. It seemed a cruel but insistent either/or. And why? So we'll find it easier to lionize the Jesuses and Siddharthas of the world if we understand how lonely they must've been?... *Yeah, good party.*

Returns Made Within 30 Days

She went home for the first time in years. So many never left, the closest compadres of her youth. She was too big for this place now. Not in a haughty way, but like a skirt from twenty pounds ago; disappointment is in the landscape. The ivy on the fences, emerald then, had dulled, and today bowed the chain link. The houses were Monopoly pieces. Maybe it had always been so and memory is merely romance. The air, stale with the odor of fixed time, touched her like groping fingers and made her yank away. Yet linger just a bit.

The Felon's Claw

He could smell her blood. Was it coming from between her legs? Or was his nose actually keen enough to glean it from her veins? The feral nature of it fed something in him. She stared at his signature, and the look of dread, unsuccessfully disguised, o'ertook her face. It was just a silly parlor trick, hawkers analyzing your handwriting at carnival booths, only meant for fun. But she'd seen something in the way he'd written his G. And as soon as he saw the look, he smelled her blood. Smelled her smelling him. Too inviting to turn away now.

Jumbo's Clown Room

They'd all chipped in for Silas' birthday lap dance. He loved claiming to prefer his women on the gamey side, to which his friends would gleefully grimace, and which pleased Silas. Jumbo's was the dive for such ilk. The stripper had serious bruising on one thigh and hair that smelled of old grease. Silas imagined her going home every dawn to a kid who was being dressed for school just as she was crawling into bed. He enjoyed picturing Bernadine's life outside of Jumbo's doors; that of human with a heart that could break, arms that held, love freely given.

Cinder

Each time he passed her window, she stared at her TV from a big chair. Sometimes she argued with it. Other times she was the quiet figure in a catatonic trance that he daily passed to get home. He never saw her cooking in her kitchen, or entertaining company. Actually, not true. He did once see another person in the window, but she and her guest never engaged with each other at all. The pair faced the television in formation and clung to the world inside the box. He could see it in their eyes, a lifeline made of cinder.

Watch Out World

Facebook Post #432: I wrote a song tonight! I've been in the longest dry spell EVER! And tonight I broke it! The gods are blessing me right now! Watch out world, I have been loosed! Facebook Post #856: I haven't written a song since. Going on five years. *Hmmm.* Maybe avoid Facebook for awhile. Or... just laugh at how much ridiculous spin we love to place on a single incident, as if it's all in preparation for that self-help book we're planning to publish. When sometimes life is just a simple head scratcher. End of story. Step, ball, change. Doodah...

Paralysis

Her to-go coffee had long gone cold. When her husband finally drove past, she sank down in her own car seat, which had parked itself several houses down. He pulled up to their house, and the sight of a woman getting out of his passenger side stabbed her. She got out of her car wielding a girl-brawling attitude, and bellowed, "Whore!" She got out of her car calmly, asking them how their evening went. She never got out of her car. Never left her crouched seat. Not even an hour later, after they'd gone inside her house, hand in hand.

Katrina

Lila loved watching Katrina entertain Frank. He was a mechanic who visited Katrina weekly, and Lila's hiding spot, during Frank's visits, was her mother's closet, door secretly ajar. Katrina's legs loved Frank's beard. Frank loved every inch of Katrina. They clung to each other as if a hurricane were about to wrench them apart; like that other Katrina that Lila had convinced herself was named after her mother, the original galeforce. Lila would practice her come-hither-ness by playing in Katrina's makeup and heels. One day she would have a Frank of her own, and master the art of hapless love.

The Gorilla Where He Lived

He was a chest-beating primate of a man. He was also one with a conscience, so he thoughtfully considered the current climate. The gorilla couldn't run free these days. And he didn't resent women for calling out men to evolve. Quite the contrary; it was about damned time. Testosterone was finally receiving its day of reckoning. But while he did his part to curtail his gorilla's bluster, it also meant there were days when this mighty roarer against the mountains and pounder of the earth just needed to go grab an axe and split a rail, to honor his quality.

Dyslexia

She stared at his vast room of heads. Antelope, deer, tigers, elk. She was repelled *and* transfixed. This man was made of the kind of fortune handed down, not earned, and he seized his day in the only way men of inheritance knew how—by covering his walls in trophies, bold statements about traveling the world and facing danger. She walked into his bathroom and noticed flowers. Leaned over to smell them and was stunned to find that they were... plastic? All she could do was mumble, eyes disgustedly rolled: "Dude. FAKE heads. REAL flowers. Not the other way around."

Doomed For a Certain Term

He was neither gifted nor charismatic enough to join the 27 Club, that cursed/blessed toggle of an age that seemed repeatedly to snatch our rock godlings from us: Hendrix, Joplin, Morrison, Cobain. Nor was he anointed enough for the 33 Club: The Prophets. Imagine walking beside Shankara and Jesus. As much as he'd longed for a bit of die-young-&-leave-a-good-looking-corpse legend attached to his own name, just the tiniest sprinkling of gravitas to make this whole trip worthwhile, he was, alas, doomed to settle for dull ordinariness and the quiet cadence and breathtaking sustain of living to a ripe old age.

Woolgatherer's Blues

The moon is low on the horizon. You're driving across CA-118, which zigzags like an obstacle course speedway around endless mountain ranges. She dances left then dances right, the moon. A partner loosed, wild. The mountains, mere silhouettes, are her rapt audience bearing secrets, though there is nothing mere in their motionless breadth against the dull dusk, and the chase is unavailing. No matter how fast your high-performance vehicle claims to be, she will out-sprint you, hiding behind ranges, peeking then ducking, playful yet elusive forever. It isn't the way you want her, but it's the way you get her.

Tormented by Hemingway

If he's never tried to die, felt the burning on the tips of his tired fingers, a gunpowder plunge from grace, he cannot write about it. If he's never killed, a raging eye for an eye, or scorned the womb that held him, he cannot dance it on a stage. If he's never lost his mind, or felt his belly swell with the hunger that he's only read about, he cannot paint it on a wall. Nor can he sing it to his artist colleagues who have all tried suicide once or twice, because they wanted to write about it.

Church Ponies

Spines arching. Hips lurching. Arms reaching. For one Sunday moment, the archipelago that is their weekday lives becomes one body, as they are hit by the Lord in a pageantry only Pentecostal churches promise. We marveled at them, the aisle stompers, usually women, imposing in their glistening coffee-skinned patina, fulfilling a kind of ancestral ecstasy that we, in our child imaginations, couldn't seem to separate from something carnal. In those imaginations, wild in their habit, we placed them on stages, giving them Klieg lights and turning them into Broadway ponies that soared high above us, wooing Heaven and Earth alike.

End-Times Adjacent

They loved each other into apoplexy, wrenching necks and declarations with near-biblical fury. Threatening to DIE, not just collapse, not crumble, not crash, not bleed, but DIE if the other dared walk away. The very act of breathing hinged on each accessing the other's dreams. A nasty haunting. No room for private thoughts. No way to walk without the tumor of their love heavily upon them. Then suddenly to feel the wind. Gentle Zephyrus carrying them away from each other, a post-apocalyptic whisper, weightless. Until inhales moved to exhales, moved to pulses slowing, moved to breathing again. Even in desolation.

Abandon Your Masterpiece: For Tom, Billie, and Dear Leonard

She was never one for pretty singing voices. If they cracked trying to reach that note, if they just barely brushed by it with a kind of brutal skid, her ears tended to perk up. If they were wretched with broken beauty (the only kind, in her book), if the souls attached to those voices were splayed across a surgeon's table, opened up, content wrung out and beaten against a wall like a dusty throw rug, she was irretrievably caught. If a $G^{\flat 6/9}$ pathos poured like syrup, it would seep within the fissures of her heart. The only ever cure.

Force Majeure

The earthquake had not yet hit, but was coming. Tragedy wouldn't be ours, as it would be others', even though the epicenter wouldn't be far, and we would take that blessing more cavalierly than we should. As we were taking everything. What we couldn't possibly know in the immediate aftermath was that the Great Northridge would form cracks and create fissures that would loosen our foundation over time, tick like a bomb beneath our feet, and one day yank us from each other in an instant. It's always something way back in the past. Some horrible jolt you simply miss.

What the End of the World Looks Like

The end of the world has happened a few times. When my father sat in our living room, my mother his co-conspirator, and told us kids they were divorcing, he'd already begun seeming like a visitor in our home before even uttering the words. When the boy I lost my virginity to didn't actually want a girlfriend, suddenly, though prior to that moment I hadn't given him a thought, I couldn't possibly fathom life without him. When Charlottesville became a nation's bellwether, and we all had a notion of what that really meant, we had to keep on breathing nonetheless.

Bokeh

She captured a cliff, a right glorious beauty. Little did she know that she was being captured. His lens caught within it a figure, a right glorious beauty, photographing cliffs. So charged was her gaze that he wondered about her cliff. Wanted to see it as she saw it. No hue imperfect. No sound out of concert with wind and gulls. No thing but it in focus. Every inch consumed with such wonder that disorientation was promised. Cliffs disoriented her. She disoriented him. Who would he disorient, in the maddening go-round of the untenable chase? And who, then, that one?

History

His paintings got locked inside her Wagoneer on a 110-degree day. Her only job had been to transport the pieces from his studio to the gallery on Traction Avenue, and she'd gotten out of the car accidentally closing the door with the keys inside. "For roadside service, expect a 45-minute wait," the phone jeered. While everyone bustled inside, readying the space for the opening, she paced curbside, staring at the paintings through dirty windows, watching their curdling demise, their cruelly random fate of making no mark on history. Meanwhile, in a room unawares, the artist prepared for his long-awaited moment.

A Perfect Illustration of the Radiant Abstract

In your absence, I smell you in the folds of curtains and the scent of trees. Hear your voice in the wind, or it calls your name. In your absence, I taste you in every succulent swallowing of wine. You are so much sweeter, I tell the wine, whose feelings I hurt. Whose wouldn't be, when told they cannot compare? In your absence, I dream you. You are standing at my door with your heart held out, saying words that make me smile again. Like a perfect illustration of the radiant abstract, my dreams will always have you coming back.

Aleatory on the Radio

Hearing "Like a Virgin" at the precise instant that she loses him gives the song a sorcery she would've bet against. It has become another kind of listening now, permanently projecting pathos onto a tenuous thread bred for jollity. This bouncy trifle will rattle her bones thence, forever done with its pap. Make itself a soldier of aleatoric notes and harrowing overtones. Pull at her ears. Stand up her hairs and unloose the bats. All because of the slaying of her husband, in her arms, by a 7-Eleven-robbing gunman blasting an early 80's pop station from his armband transistor radio.

Language

He never spoke to us. She did. She was kind. Sang songs. Read us stories. He buried his head in the crosswords, tenaciously mute, maybe a grumble while reading the paper, but keeping his taciturn distance. I always wondered why he never engaged with Brother and me. After our first overnight stay at Auntie and Ol' Mister's, we quickly learned why never engaging was best. As he angrily flung the coffee table to get at her, amid our terrified child screams, we realized that this too—a fist to her face, a shattered mirror, a deep pain erupting—was language.

Sleight of Hand

Between the Chinese linking rings and the levitating cards, Trevor bedded his conquest. He had taken her upstairs, amid the storage inventory of his magic shop, and had found a clump of drapery, probably a magician's curtain, on which to lay her down. Anonymity had been her one condition. She'd come in to buy some easy magic tricks that she could learn for her daughter's first birthday party. But Trevor could see in her lingering that she was looking for something else, and he considered himself the man for the job. "Can you teach me the disappearing trick?" she asked.

Life

An acrid suit coat run stiff from the years of sweat. His liquored flesh, a pustuled leather. The neighborhood wino. Terminal heartbreak, not to mention the alcohol, had gotten him years ago, and he bemoans a life unrealized and much too long. *Why can't I die already?* But when little Rodney is hit by the speeding joyriders, Ol' Mister is as upright as the man he was at thirty. They'll never stop talking about the day he was Jesse Owens, swooping the neighbor child into the cradle of his crusty sleeve, and breathed life back. Little Rodney's. And Ol' Mister's.

Trajectory

She fed us kids homemade cupcakes every Sunday after church, while she and our mother shared a pot of tea. She was the warm, sugary center of my childhood. I saw her recently, galumphing down Ventura Boulevard wearing the armor we all know well—flesh and rags the hard hue of steely charcoal. My heartbeat pummeled my chest, as I tried to get her to remember me. When I offered her money, she snatched it and stormed off, cursing into the wind. I broke. But something in her had broken years ago, and who knows why. Who ever knows why?

The Day I Became a Haunting

I slipped on the wet ground. Fell in the well. A hundred feet down for a hundred years. I shrieked to be noticed. A pile of broken bones. But no one heard me. No one paused. Only feet moving above me. Bustling, harried paces. Dancing on my head. Sensing an echo. They think it's their pain screaming at them. But it's only me. A lingering wraith. Unable to put my own pain to bed until they all successfully undo themselves for their deeds. And then the day when I can finally rest. It's coming. I feel it. Any moment now.

Finding Ivy

Little Ivy went in for a hernia operation, bunking in a ward with twenty screaming children. She didn't know anyone, so she screamed too. Calming down only when she was brought alphabet soup, Ivy pulled the bowl to her mouth, and dribbled half of it down her front, undiscovered until weeks later when the bandages were removed and pieces of moldy peas and carrots and letters that spelled *mlgeekba* were found pasted to her stomach. She'd hated being in the hospital, but when her "predicament" made the doctor laugh, little Ivy was officially hooked on the conceit of being weird.

Naked

Masked gunmen burst into the party and had everyone strip down so their valuables could be looted. She was more mortified of being naked than she was of being killed. As she looked around the frightened room, at each horrified face, what struck her most (clearly the shock) was that this conceit was a bit like telling one's story. That if we are brave enough to be shed, a remarkable unburdening has the chance to occur. And by that, not only are we unburdened, but to each other connected. Sure would be nice if she didn't have to die tonight.

The Violet Hours

They hawked snake's blood and deer penis wine as aphrodisiacs, and when he looked up he caught some bestiality porn blaring on a television behind a counter. Why Taipei's night market drew him he couldn't decipher. He lived a regular American life with a loving wife who gave him loads of room, though he never took the room because it just felt like a can of worms. Snake Alley was one of those cans, and he would never survive it if he allowed even one worm's escape. He was drawn to these hours. Not the sweet trifles of day. This.

There Are No Others

We built forts and put our toys inside. You reminded me of this as we passed a homeless man buried within his. You didn't notice him, yet it couldn't've been coincidence that you brought up our childhood pastime at that precise moment. Do I ever sense the nearness of something, even as it doesn't consciously register, only to then conjure a memory? A subconscious connection between us and them? A most definite answer to the question: How do we regard others? Perhaps a way of fueling our humanity when everything else around us says to ignore, distance, build a wall?

A Sunday Afternoon on the Island of La Grande Bot

As he walked the streets of Shibuya, with the blinding glare of harsh fluorescence shooting out from every storefront of every game arcade, the tinnitus-like hum of the machines hypnotized him even as he fought with everything in him to stay present, see beauty, breathe deeply. There was no nature for miles, nothing remotely hinting at anything organic. Just a vertigo spin of LED, nanoparticles, cryptocurrency, and injections of something resembling Freon into vaguely bio veins. He couldn't even remember paintings and music and the people who made them. They still existed though, right? That promise was all he had.

On Top of the World

He'd brokered a brilliant deal for her, and before she knew it they were on a plane to Tokyo. The meeting went spectacularly. Later, in the hotel elevator, she breathed for the first time in days, not wanting to jinx anything but whispering excitedly, "We're on top of the freaking world, aren't we?" "We sure are, darlin'," he smiled. When the KS lesions on his arms got noticed, he quickly covered, countering her stare. "Just fell... so clumsy," he tossed away, as he got off at his floor, winking the wink of old uncles promising that everything's gonna be alright.

Ensō

The tiny woman crouched in her garden and was still, hands lotioned in soil, head bowed to the near ground, back facing the world, spine protruding scoliotic like raised welts, ancient but agile, a sculpture. Enveloped in camellias, willows, azaleas, she knelt beside a cascade, water trickling down from the east, rilling over stones. The garden sat in the midst of bustling Yokohama, yet untouched by its flurry. A couple strolled, not far, holding hands, in love and new. They passed by. Slowed to contemplate the woman. "Do you think she's planting seeds, or meditating?" asked he. "Yes," said she.

Trinkets

Tanya brought him back to her motel room across the street from the bar. He was way too drunk to get it up, but it was never about that. This time she'd scored an actual groom, as in, still in his tuxedo. She wanted to find his unlucky bride, show her what a pig her new husband was, and tell her to run for the hills. Tanya tugged his cummerbund and felt the queer triumph that on a couple's wedding night she was the one chosen, a charm in her pocket, more gleaming than the treasonous gold around his finger.

Frames

The 405 hypnotized tonight. Everything moved like lovers. It was just the rarest of interludes that did not include the wall of metal and exhaust usually dousing the canvas of new road. The five-year-long Caltrans project was supposed to ease the congestion. It never did. But this time of night, passing the giant neon G of the Galleria off the Ventura exit actually serenaded him as he made his way over the hill to home. Serenaded him almost as sweetly as the John Coltrane playlist seeping out of his JBL speakers. Trane and the 405 at midnight. A luscious rendezvous.

A Word

You died. You died and you couldn't tell me. That night a few months ago when we texted each other through an entire movie? I don't have unlimited texting; it cost me a fortune. But we laughed ridiculously that night, and even then not a word. So then I think, well, maybe it was an unexpected thing, until I read something about *"...after a long illness."* I don't know why it matters, but it does. A word I could've said, something to let you know I loved you. Now you're dead, and you don't know that. Death is so selfish.

Dog and Six Order the Número Seis

Dogwood Poe and Sixsmith Siqueiros ordered the Número Seis and a champurrado at La Luz del Dia. They'd been ordering the #6 for fifty years, sitting at the same uneven table that overlooked the plaza, and debating art, politics, and the social order. Dog revered revolutionaries, agitators. While Six believed in the philosophy of a cooperative society as the only true freedom from tyranny. About the only thing they agreed on was that Luz's handmade tortillas had never once failed the standards of two old cowboy compadres and their lust for all things intellectual. The Número Seis was their touchstone.

Spilled Milk

With the milk carton still clutched by a hand frozen from shock, he lay in his own blood, which turned pink from the immersion of spilled milk. He was another black boy taken down. In his last breaths, he saw the headlines, the outcry from a tragically necessary movement, the litany that would now include his name. Even over seeing the faces of his mother, father, little brother, the unspeakable affliction that was about to be theirs, or the milk errand that would never make it back home to the nuclear family that Today's America had no interest in knowing.

En Plein Air

Did hers count? She'd asked herself that question for years. It wasn't until the world seemed to erupt—starting in Hollywood, and anyone's guess where it might end—that she felt her voice slowly begin to tiptoe out of hiding, after all the years of being mute. The smeary lines she could never make clear. The belief in her own complicity. The take-no-prisoners reckoning that was presently happening as women (and men) more courageous than she were stepping forward in droves, inspiring the most explosive hashtag in internet history, braved the harsh conditions of an uncontrolled environment, producing the masterpiece.

Hug Machines

The movies are perfect. No one talks to me in the darkened room, but they're there. Crucial bubble wrap, keeping me from breaking. A restaurant is perfect. My head buried in a good book, unbothered, while the collective inhales and exhales encircle me like dancing cigarette smoke. The city is perfect. Behind windows, I listen to Elliott Smith and early Miles, meditate, drink rum, binge-watch *Sherlock*, and don't answer the phone when it rings, but am assured that the world outside—traffic, kisses, collisions, arguments, beating hearts—wraps around me like a favorite blanket that keeps the chill at bay.

Break Me In Half

Shatter me into pieces. Make my left do what my right won't. Swing the wrecking ball into my staid lines and mundane ligatures until they crack and skip like a record needle. Let the needle fall onto foreign shores, snowy summits, untrodden grooves, stabbing and smarting too scared flesh, too comfortable tomorrows. The cracks will fill in with a permeable marrow, the bones grown stronger at the breaks. And time will keep its promise anyway. So pull at my seams. Bust me wide open. Let me not suffocate, smothered in bubble wrap and shadow, skittish to the taste of daring.

The Dinner Party

She was the consummate hostess. Impeccable detail to a fault. Her husband asking her for a divorce but minutes before the first guests arrived threatened a stain upon the landscape of her perfect dinner party. She never lost the smile, the enthusiastic inquiry into her guests daily lives, the witty banter for which she was known. Beneath the banter quivered a rejected heart, thready and torn, newly pummeled with a timing suspiciously cruel, yet still she maneuvered masterfully the crucial art of giving her guests her all. Meanwhile, her husband's feigned jollity betrayed a look, a spark, a damned twinkle.

The Dead Man's Shoes

He stole the shoes off a dead man that he came across in an alley. Slipped them on, tied the laces, felt the leather grip his frozen toes. After so many nights bare and numb, his feet were finally warm. Hands feeling the soft skin of a woman. Tasting her sweat. The hairs standing on end. Almost there, *almost!* The knife swiftly in his back. Blood spreading. He walked around in the shoes the entire night, trying to see what else might flash, what other secrets might leak out. The dead man could no longer speak. His Bruno Maglis, however...

Ommmm

The world was caving in. She climbed a mountain that overlooked wide swaths of green valley, searching for redemption. Sitting to meditate, the wind gentle on her face, heart heavy, she welcomed the quiet. When out of the blue, quiet vanished, as the happiest Labrador puppy on the planet rambunctiously laid her flat, slathering her from head to toe in spittle. He'd simply decided, as her laughter became inconsolable, that she was not allowed to hurt anymore today. Then, like all the greatest angels and bodhisattvas, off Giant Puppy gallivanted to find his next victim and anoint with unruly love.

Calluses

He has developed calluses. Calluses to protect him from the beasts. The beasts that object to his race. The beasts that try to tell him whom he can love. The beasts that render him invisible as he enters old age. The beasts that weigh in on his beauty. His status. There's a callus for every damned beast in captivity. Every season, every climate. He is an armor of calluses. A heavy, scaly armor built to weather any storm, but with a limited warranty. Oh, what he wouldn't give to trade in that armor for a robe made of flowing muslin.

She Was Twelve

Patty was twelve, and all her friends talked about the sex they were having. She didn't know whether to believe them, but couldn't imagine it. They called it *loony crunching*, which, even to her twelve-year-old self, sounded too childish to fit the discomfiting subject. If they were lying, then she wondered if she shouldn't lie too. A certain strut was required to wear the claim, truth or not. Patty was too old for the dolls she still loved, and too young for this—a terrifying limbo that had her retreating to her Barbie universe, where she needn't strut at all.

Querencia

You draw your closed eyes toward the lit candle, hands in añjali mudrā, careful to sense the flame as it nears, as you do your closing meditation bow, still deciding if it's to Source within you, outside of you, or merely in your stardust wishes. Was it the Buddha or the Christ that tapped you today? One of the Great Teachers always does. Even some dude you encountered who said a throwaway thing that shook you. You open eyes. Stare at the flame. Blow. Watch it Watusi like a Pentecostal, then vanish. The rest of the day is always better.

The Barely-Trail

I passed a young woman in the woods on the barely-trail. She stopped as we passed and called out my name, a wisp of air through the copse. When I turned, no one was there. Only her dress, clumped on the dirted ground, the smell of mothballs and White Shoulders Perfume. An antique hairbrush lay beside it, with tangles of black strands that began to encircle my hands and strangle my arms like a fast-creeping ivy. "Grandmother," I whispered. She, who'd been the only one in my family to untangle her pain through poetry, often haunted me. "Stay," I begged.

Regrets Large and Small Taste Bitter All the Same

It was the evening of his execution. They were allowed to spend the day with him in a common room, and the family just sat together, silent, him in wrist-&-leg irons. These would be the most precious hours he had left, but she fell asleep on his shoulder (barely even allowed) and nobody bothered to nudge her. When time was up, he roused her by whispering: "They're here for me, baby girl. Time to say goodbye." *Nooooo!* He was executed six hours later. Every bit of it would haunt her, and she would forever wonder if he regretted *his* crime.

Foot Fetish

Gently my feet he washed. The act, pregnant with reverence. As if he took into account my walking the labyrinth, barefoot, clutching my candle, setting intentions, a darkened room, and one by one, as each person placed their candle somewhere on its path, the labyrinth emerged illumined, our prayers held inside. Or my walking over hot coals, a field of 10,000 people and the night sky, the fevered promise of possibility, feeling the white heat of burning embers, yet emerging victorious, unharmed, heart expanded, bare feet the glowing warm conduit of something holy. By his expression, he felt it too.

Lurid

The dirty needle was the cleanest thing between them. He loved the look on every sucker's face whenever she finessed a con, while she loved the tortured soul his writer's lot had birthed, and the bottle that seemed compulsory to the deed. When he found her slumped in the tub, foaming in places one shouldn't, the romance of the lurid wrested right out of Louis, that his sweet Ridley would give no hint to her intended out. Now he sat nightly at the Norms that allowed him hours nursing cold coffee, toiling to scribble even the limpest words about her.

Love

When she asked it, love reigned over her. Made her mindful. Gave her grace. Delivered her from need. Filled her with wonder. Urged her to daring. Spurred her to service. Helped her to stillness. Compelled her to live fully in the present while steadfastly tending the gentle ground of her life's purpose. Then love taught her to let go of every ask, every beg, so that she might simply bear witness to life as it bloomed in bursts and rains of sundry light. She counted herself lucky that love was willing, patiently and doggedly, to reteach her this every day.

Brush

He eyed a couple on the street kissing, too deliciously meretricious for public view. He was drawn to the windshield glass in the street, shattered into snow, the splats of red upon it, the ubiquitous yellow tape. He was irretrievably snagged by a crosswalk box so layered with graffiti that it transcended its civic role and became art. Seeing wonder where others saw nothing unusual was his proudest gift. Which only added woeful insult to the injury that he hadn't left his house in years until today. He felt hopeful for a next brush, a next magnificent interception with life.

Coyote

1969. Coyote was a boy from the neighborhood. He was never without a joke in his pocket and always the life of the party. One day Coyote went away. None of us kids knew where, or why. The grown folk thought they were protecting us with their talk of his absence in hushed whispers. Instead, we were spooked. *Is he dead? No one will tell us anything!* Then one day Coyote reappeared. We excitedly awaited a joke, but there was no light within. Coyote was no longer Coyote. And while the grown folk celebrated his return, we felt only death.

Two Gentlewomen of West Hollywood

As ladies-in-waiting in a five-hour production of Hamlet, they had loads of time in between their scenes (so much of the damned thing fixated on the damned Dane), so they routinely wandered down the street to grab a pint at Barney's Beanery, fully costumed in their Elizabethan monstrosities. They weren't looked at twice ordering Guinness like something out of a Bill & Ted adventure. By the time they returned for their next scenes, they were properly tanked, and acted their asses off, even throwing out a few ad-libbed lines. Total blasphemy. Hell, they had plenty of years to learn taste.

Little Marcus Finds God

The blood of Christ was an irresistible Welch's Grape Juice. The body, saltines. We didn't do wine and wafers, like the Catholics. We did it in a way that made me wanna get religion real quick. I was a boy of ten, with appetites. I couldn't quite contain myself whenever it was time for Holy Communion, and my parents got to drink that grapey lusciousness but I couldn't because I wasn't yet baptized. My nose always caught the fruity whiff, like a candied fever. I doubt I'd've ever found God had I been raised across the street at St. Catherine's.

The United States' Most Distinguished Veteran

Professor Ernest Lee got on the bus, sporting his best cravat and walking stick, cherished gifts from the Sultan. When he chatted up a young woman who sat beside him, he offered her his business card. Dogeared from having lived in his musty breast pocket forever, he was nonetheless proud of its content: *"Philosopher, Athlete, Inventor, Screenplaywriter, Baritone, Composer, Educator, Scholar, Astronaut, Original Thinker, and The United States' Most Distinguished Veteran."* He looked excitedly for a reaction and took her pursed lips for a smile. He quite liked this one, so it was a shame hers was the next stop.

And Thus She Considers the Precious Beasts

I stare from the taverna window onto a street strewn with semen and piss if I'm really paying attention, sipping a wicked Turkish coffee. Across this bacterial minefield lies Hamburg's Herbertstraße, a most notorious alley. I always seem inclined toward a city's red-light district. Quicksilver shoots from my pupils onto the billboarded entrance that reads *"frauen verboten."* I want to push against this outmoded androcentrism with every muscle in my righteous indignations. I want to fall inside one of its prostitute's self-worth and walk in her shoes. I want to understand the debaucheries of men. I never do, of course.

Tyranny

The car drove by him in the alley, and he caught her eye. There'd been the day when his good looks had been able to snag them like that, with a charm and a wink. Today she caught him in his moment alone, unable to hold his urine as he confusedly tried to figure out how his pants worked, and uncertain of where he was. When he saw the recipe of horror and pity on her passing face at the wetness spreading across his front, he danced a bit to camouflage his indignities, cursing the tyranny of a man's decline.

Road Rash

He opened the door and frightened me. Exploding muscles tore at his flesh. I asked for Doris, and he escorted me into a squalid living room where his mother sat in a slobbered stupor. She needed to give me urine for the insurance. It would be useless if she was tanked, but this job was so dispiriting I wasn't about to return later. I followed her to the bathroom. After awhile, I knocked and knew she'd passed out on the can. Muscles was staring me down. Best to keep my gaze anywhere else. The battle scars were starting to itch.

The Incredible Shrinking Woman

She regularly found ways to chop everyone down at the knees. Just the tiniest comment, cutting to the bone, but always with a smile to stamp her innocence. It was her way of keeping people, especially fellow women (the saddest of her sins), smaller than her. She shuddered at the notion of her own smallness. Yet in all her machinations to grow taller than the rest, she only grew in the opposite direction, never realizing that it was she, herself, who put those wheels in motion, with her incredible shrinking potion, stirred with a dash of bitters and a brandish.

Cataracts

He was starting to lose all memory of every book he'd ever read and loved. These stories, which could always be counted on to conquer the malaise of his life with their rich and variegated horizons, were largely smearing away from his remembrances, and all that seemed left were splotches of dull color. "Oh this muted red smudge here seems to be a dystopian horror that vaguely deconstructs bureaucracy." "And this grayish-purple stain here, this, I think, has something to do with a rape trial in the south. Or is it a murder in Saint Petersburg?" And so it began.

Dukes

Her brothers showed her how to "put her dukes up," as they used to say. And for years she started envisioning her whole body covered in her warrior dukes; a fantasia that required the possession of many more than the customary pair of fists appendaging from each arm. Her body was a spreading virus of dukes, growing out of every cranny, orifice, every pocket of flesh. The two largest fists sprouted, respectively, from her vagina and the center of her chest. When she bled monthly, it seeped between the hundreds of white-knuckled fingers, droplets of vigilance, until safety was sworn.

MVP

Baseball was in his blood. Tryouts with the MLB and mentoring by a Major League pitcher, his was a promising career cut short by bad knees, the same ones that kept him out of active duty. But when something was in his blood, he wasn't about to shake it off just because the body had its limits, so he started coaching Little League. For the rest of his life, the man who would never father a child of his own became exactly that to the multitude of youngsters for whom the game was often a venting ground for troubled childhoods.

An Odyssey for Alice Cotu

Alice Cotu could lay hands on, take away your cancer, your blues, your lascivious impulses. She softened what was brick, strengthened what was ash. She never took money for her gifts, and she never spoke, incapable of social interaction. Her shaman powers were given to her that long ago winter, the bleakest of them, when she'd spent its entirety alone in an abandoned farmhouse, a mere child. The isolation had nearly rendered her feral. Today devotees traveled from around the world just to be healed by Alice's touch, never knowing the price exacted, but always a sense of her secrets.

Old Things New

I waited forever for you. Through heartbreak and ruin. Through moments of weakness that could've used your thumb beneath my chin. Through victories that needed your cheers. Then you came. After a lifetime of surrogates and placeholders you arrived, and we made each other, old things, new again. I was a kind of person when we met. That person won't always be apparent, but cling to her, I beseech. She is here, if at times buried. I'll do the same for you. When the fresh dirt covers those aspects, and shaking off is needed, let us recover, and never recover.

Sentience

As a child, she romped the fields with a hundred piggies, feeding and playing with them in the mud. Their squeals were song, and she swam in the song, until it was time to help shear the angoras. The babies yielded the best mohair, brilliant for use on handcrafted dolls, the kind that won her ribbons at fairs. Today she wrestled with a world that refused toothbrushes and soap to detained migrant children, a world that rounded them up like chattel, tossing off, with impunity, words like *wrangle* and *herd*, words that should only ever be familiar to farm life.

It's Been Years

I walk in and find that the boy I loved as a girl has grown hard, done time, lost teeth, battled demons. His father, my teacher and mentor, lies in a hospital bed, unable to feel his left arm. The man who once laid brilliant hands on a piano and upended my world can barely lay hands anywhere anymore. I can't cry in front of people. Were I able, I wonder if he'd realize it meant love, not pity. Stroke, they say. And the son? Just hard life. I wonder what they see in me that they no longer recognize.

Delicato

The church bells that chimed gloriously at their wedding. The bluebells he planted for her in their garden, her favorites. The jingle bells of their first Christmas together with the twins, a family at last. The alarm bells that sounded beneath his solar plexus when she grew distant. The intercom bell that buzzed them in to see their therapist, as they held hands, uncertain. The siren's bell that pulsated as the ambulance took her away. The electrocardiograph bell that hummed a lacerating $F^\sharp$ as she flatlined, too fragile for this world. The passing bell tolling its goodbye, a family undone.

Annihilation

Downward Dog used to be so easy. Or maybe she was just never doing it right. Was she now? Because right now Mercy could barely be in the asana without it feeling like a painful purge. The thing about any kind of transformational practice was that you usually felt broken before you felt whole. The teacher eased everyone into Shavasana, where you simply lie there. But lying there meant being there, and being in Mercy's life at present was a bit like choppy seas. Yoga had never been about beautiful bodies serening out. For Mercy, it was a holy bloodletting.

The Music Lover

He loved music so much that it was only a matter of time before he'd fixate on the makers of it. He was an audience mainstay at every jazz joint that featured burning musicians. He wanted to be their friend so badly, he couldn't quite help himself when one of them finally told him to back off and he came back later wielding a shiv. Bar patrons were unsuccessful in tackling him before his chance to strike. "Would you like a refill?" asked the bartender, snapping him out of a reverie that had completely drowned out the music he loved.

Her Loveliest Trait

The corridor of the Musée d'Orsay was a vast, echoey chamber. I stood before the 150-year-old painting in an upstairs salon. The hairs stood up. My mother had been right. It was ME in the painting. A field as atmospheric as Millet could occasion. A shepherdess and her flock. Downward gaze of fleshy cheek and sullen eyes. In fact, no eyes at all, just eyelids. Mine. My whimsical mother could never resist a merry penchant for spinning magical fables—her loveliest trait, frankly—and had insisted that I'd been that shepherdess in another lifetime, inspiring Jean-François, perhaps even his lover.

The Rooftops of Paris

The rooftops of Paris held all his dreams atop. If the wind shifted just so, one would flit away like a feather, bouncing and dipping, landing somewhere else altogether; say, one of the gargoyles of Notre-Dame, or the ledge of Pont Neuf, ready to take on new adventures. The kid had not one ounce of irony in him, so he earnestly suffused upon his dreams the very magic that only feathers and Paris rooftops could promise. He perpetually heard muted trumpets, captured raindrops on his tongue, and lived for knowing that falling in love was always just around the corner.

Her

The rains have stopped but not the chill. I can't check into the hotel yet because my room won't be ready until 11am. That's four hours away, and I don't know the city. With luggage in tow, I take off on foot. I've no clue what part of town I'm in, as the kiosks begin opening up. I turn a gray corner and am suddenly halted in my awed tracks. What a hackneyed cliché—*finding refuge from the cold in an old church*—and one I have absolutely zero intentions on resisting, as the astonishing Notre-Dame beckons me to her.

Better Days

Her skin was as black as pitch, bones gnarled and protuberant. The ribbons on her bobby socks hung limply. She'd seen better days. His skin was the color of an elephant's tusk. He sported his pork pie hat, a hip replacement limp, and a bouquet of roses always. He'd seen better days. When the music started, they vamped onto the platform, her twirling that girlish skirt, him brandishing that bouquet like a pistol. The dance floor awaited their nightly footprint, heated up, and expanded upon their descent. The roses never survived a night. It was the very best of days.

Sisters

She and Sister could always feel each other's pains. Knew each other's joys instinctively, even before getting the good news. Heard one another's cries. Smelled each other's fears. Tasted each other's triumphs, like the best monkey bread drenched in butter. They could fight furiously, like any two, but could never be rid. Theirs was a tie such that both, separately and unknowingly, died at the exact same moment, each deeply sensing the other's passage, bringing a desperately needed symmetry to a world much too heartlessly aleatoric and out of sync, and giving the whole painting a light worthy of Turner.

Will

She was not prophetic. Not a mystic. It was one of her most
disappointing self-resolves. She never sensed someone dying or
tragedy striking. She had earth-mamas all around her who did. Not
her. But when she wet her bed for the first time since childhood, she
waited, alarmed, for the sign. A ring of the phone. A rude knocking
at the door announcing the incident. A shamanistic explanation for
her disturbing sleeptime incontinence. She refused to be the pitiful
who now suffers enuresis. She, instead, insisted upon being the sage
who operates in ways no one understands but everyone awes.

Grace Notes

She met the actor Richard Jordan at a party when she was a young actress trying to break into films. He walked up to stand beside her while she stared at a journalistic-style black & white photograph of an elderly homeless woman bathing off the edge of a shallow peer. She sensed the actor's presence (*Interiors* was his!) and murmured, "It's beautiful, isn't it?" "Is it?" he returned. "I think it's a staged lie." He pointed, with an examination she lacked. "See how no one else in the shot is noticing her? Wouldn't happen." She quit acting the next day.

Five Epistolaries and a Teacher

Dearest Sir *(Student I)*

Keep on being a prick, if you must. Plenty have also been geniuses, history can affirm. Though what I really wish for you is that you can find your way toward treasuring your humanity over your genius, if a choice must be made, and if the chase is what's gotten in the way. There was absolute gold in your lessons, if also abuse and a bitterness for never being given your due. I am grateful for the artist I am because of you. But I pray every day that I never give it a more auspicious pedestal than being whole.

Dearest Sir *(Student II)*

You completely upended my life. I recall you having us read a passage from a novel you deemed brilliant (you deemed so few that). You asked us to identify the protagonist in this war between two characters, and while most of us named one or the other, the rest cleverly claiming both, you eventually revealed for us that the fog itself (for this reader just an atmospheric shading of scene) was the true protagonist. I've never read books the same way again. You are an utter original in how you look at the written word, and I am forever indebted.

Dearest Sir *(Student III)*

It seems only yesterday that I, and others, collapsed beneath the tide of your criticisms aimed at shaping the artist, if not the work. Do you ever sleep? Knowing the spines crushed for art's sake? The weapons wielded to bolster? Not us but you? You call your dirty fighting building bones, your lonely world made less so only by the babies in your care who clamor to you, hoping for abuse to mean love. For rage to mean passion. Hoping to please. What we didn't know was that pleased isn't in your lexicon. Pleased is for suckers. Pleased means death.

Dearest Sir *(Student IV)*

The pearls you gave, hard won from your own mountain climbed, what a gift. Was it a sacrifice? Did some chunk of you get chewed away in order to share it with us, a mother pre-masticating for her babies? I feel privileged to have been snapped in two—the only way to multiply is to divide—to have felt the bludgeoning tool against my pretty stories that took the world nowhere, that merely staved off fears awhile. Privileged to see the world through its prism shards, smarting as shards do. What is it all for, otherwise? This you taught us.

Dearest Sir *(Student V)*

Your novel is a work of art. It could easily be likened to the Victor Hugos and Dostoevskys of the world. But you will never be likened to them, because you will never finish your beautiful opus and put it out there. I have come to realize that perhaps that doesn't necessarily have to be everyone's end point. Perhaps for you this novel is redemption. And your intention might well be to keep that process alive and ongoing as your vehicle for purging demons. I guess that's as good a reason as any. So, be well, dearest sir. Break open.

Shed

I cut off all my hair, a river of beguiling braids. Had my implants removed after years endowed. Stared into the mirror and wondered if the world still considered me a woman. Did my societal armor of salines, weaves, and acrylic nails make the woman? Or did it just make theatre? A clever deflection from the fleshly imperfections of a woman in the gloaming of her days? I rather like to think it might be my heart, my soul, undisguised in the shedding, that defines me. A girl can dream. A girl can grow hair in unsightly places, and dream.

Betrayal

She sat a row away. The smell was overwhelming, and I felt cruel thinking it. The sour putrefaction of having endured the streets for years, the salt-rot hijacking of flesh and sometimes mind. It's only right that she get to come in from the cold for a bit. Get some artistic nourishment in the bargain. The cost, a movie ticket. I go to movies alone. So does she. I withstood the smell because it felt cruel not to. After all, I get the luxury of anonymity, without the billboard of my unsympathized plight worn on me, a cloak of betrayal.

Blood

As we passed the cotton field, my stepfather explaining its significance, we pulled off the highway, a sobering diversion from our planned family vacation itinerary, and exited the RV to pick a few bolls. I found out years later that a debate had ensued over the efficacy of electing us kids to experience a swatch of our ancestors' slavery plight. But I got it. If not at the time, certainly later on. It's one thing to read of history in a book. Quite another to have your brutalized fingers, from the spiky task, forever after experience a deeply ancestral painbody.

A Clutch of Strong Flowers

Because the rains came and I began to wonder if they'd ever stop, because Los Angeles honestly got barely a taste of what other climes consider normal yet I framed the unusual occurrence with my usual sounding of the alarm bells, because the rains came and stayed longer than I was comfortable with, the white jacarandas have lined every street like a formation of angel warriors, the painted ladies have stormed the village in search of their north, and the whole unfamiliar eruption of staggering wildness has stolen the absolute heart of a woman who has tended to hate rain.

The Writing On the Wall

While house hunting, they walked into a dilapidated Victorian that showed restoration promise. The phone numbers etched erratically on every inch of wall, and not a single one duplicated (this discovered after she went about the obsessive task), should've alerted them to an existing force. He tossed it off as the hypergraphia of a mad former occupant. But she knew. She couldn't tell him that the Ghost of Crazy Past was not what *she* feared; it was the scrawls' tease and calling of a mania that grazed its fingers up her arm, whispered her name, told her she was home.

This Train

I escape by train from Paris to Nice. It's all I can do to elope to this Nice (or Paris) I've created, where no one is sick or dying. When I arrive (is it Paris or Nice now? I've lost my way), I'm too afraid to exit this train. Exiting means committing. To taking on France, who'll help me run away. I happily give France a pronoun. She's clearly a She. Italy would be male, of course. But I am too offending to make it to San Remo. It was all I could do just to get on this train.

Under Water

Instead of honoring a ritual by which he nightly prepared for bed, then awakened in the morning refreshed by the sunrise, he would fall off every single dark of morning to the white noise and blue wash of the television, after having fought with everything in him to stave off sleep. The waking hours were a desperate drug, with the threat of noiseless abyss if his eyes dared shut. Perhaps even the fear of never waking up again, rendering each night's theoretical final passage not one of beauty or meaning, but of the fading gray stupor of a life underwater.

Dirty Girl

In talking on the struggles of depression, her friend confessed to Dirty Girl Syndrome. She hadn't heard the term before, but instantly understood. The inability, when alarm is in the gut. When the film builds up, creating crucial armor. When the stink of one's failures insists on being metaphorized by literal stink. But does the brain really operate like poetry? Or is this just a case of insisting poignancy on wounds for the sake of oxygen in the face of shame? In the face of her friend's courage, she found her own end of the conversation to be quite quiet.

The Knacker's Yard

He came home unexpectedly. Sneaked into his mother's house in the middle of the night. His sister was still awake, reading by candlelight. When he saw her, he poured everything to her in a night whisper. Their parents would disown him, he knew, but he just couldn't do the armed thing, the war thing, the killing-as-abstract thing. He couldn't. His very soul had been emptied out on those front lines. Irrevocably, he feared. No one would ever understand, and dishonorable discharge meant ruin. His sister hugged him forcefully. "When you start to feel like you're nothing, just hold onto this."

Reflections of a 15-Year-Old Torch Singer Wannabe

I escaped my parents' hotel room somewhere after midnight and got myself to the Village. A New York virgin. Poking my head into several jazz clubs, all percolating in a way unfamiliar to this smalltown girl, where midnights were somnolent at best, I picked one that I figured was my best shot at sitting in. The piano player never even asked my key. Or my age. After singing "Misty," enveloped in cigarette smoke and blue velvet allure, a fantasia my girlfriends didn't share, I hastened back to Central Park, beyond reeling, in a taxi that cloistered all my possibilities inside.

Ecclesia (The Gathering of Those Summoned)

Following diagnosis, he followed his agitated heart. It took him to the pier underpass where Pops and Poet lived. Dancer Girl lived there too. She painted his face and pierced his ear, and under the city moon they found God and each other. He gave away every bit of clothing he owned except what was on his back. Better that Pops, who may've been near ninety, and wheel-chaired, have the expensive fleece coat than his young back. His whole world had opened up and he felt his purpose. No one from his official life got it. No one needed to.

Throwing Clay

Ruin is the road to transformation, the great teachers have told me time and again. What constitutes ruin? Am I ruined if I lose every bit of material worth I've ever had? If I commit the greatest sins my soul defines? If I leave dreams in the dust and opt for coma instead? If I am a lizard yearning to be a leaf? Shaking off the skin I was born to, the cells that built me, throwing clay to be reshaped? Spinning until dizziness collapses me to the ground? Spitting and purging until new form takes shape, and shape takes?

Breast Cancer Awareness on Ruffner Ave

She came upon the stop sign while doing her morning jog. Someone had spray-painted over the word *stop* and replaced it with *tits*. It looked like a simple case of mischievous taggers, inspiring laughter, until she saw the tiny pink ribbons hanging on the adjacent fence. What fearlessness it took to do a midnight run with paint can in hand for such a mission. She could never be that ballsy. It was art, in all the right ways. When it was "corrected" the next day (city government on it, for once), it made her sad. For it, and for her.

The Artist

He strolled the gallery, awaiting greatness, or at least the acknowledgment of greatness. The buzz was palpable. Then he started to panic. *Female Nude Rising* wasn't ready yet. *Abstract #5* needed tweaks. They would discover his secrets. As much as he believed in art that did exactly that, he wasn't ready for his own to be lain on the slab quite yet. Let someone else be pounded into ground round tonight. He started snatching canvases off the walls. The police were called. He was next day's news. Fodder for the gossip mill. No one talked about the art at all.

Mabel and Moses

They were a greasy old couple with guitars as greasy as them. They had greasy singing voices too. His was a crunchy grease, like good fried chicken. Hers, more of a syrupy grease, best for soppin' up with a biscuit. They often busked near the West Bottoms, greasing up their blues so greasy that B.B. King would slap his mama. I've pretty much spent my life trying to avoid grease, especially when it comes to, say, fast food, or hair. But after having these two shatter me, I've discovered I prefer my blues dripping, igniting, and burning down the kitchen.

Ashes Over Dust

When I die, there will be no dignity in it. My mouth will gape open. I may even lose my bowels. And when my newly formed ghost-self looks back on all the dances danced for bodily perfection, she'll laugh, because no matter who represented flawlessly in life, we'll all die the same way, body parts ceasing their function, degrading into the earth, ashes over dust. Then again, to go the way of the warrior's heap, jostled, spent, and thrashed for having thrown ourselves into the ring of life with nothing to lose, may just be the most dignified hand played.

Deadpan Sam

She walks into the sanctuary much too early in the morning, after a rough Saturday night of gigging late. With a 7-Eleven coffee in hand, she greets the church musicians in order to rehearse for Sunday service, handing them copies of her music for a song called "Mantra Bliss." Thinking she might get a chuckle from the guys, considering the title, she'd scribbled on the sheet music, *repeat till there's world peace*, with a smiley face. Upon reading the instruction out loud, Sam, the music director, without missing a beat, retorts: "Sure. As long as you can guarantee the overtime."

Audacious

Last night I dreamed I was audacious and left the city behind. Swapped out the little black dresses of my entertainment trade for flea market frocks. Went to bed at dusk and awoke at first light, instead of the vampire hours that often saw the other end of the emerging dawn, a gothic canvas of unwashed mascara. Breathed more deeply because I no longer had to fit into the tiny box (or outfit) my former industry had required of me. God, I'm glad it was only a dream. How I love getting older in a town cruelest in that department.

Inheritance

From Father she learned to hot-wire a car, change a battery, bleed the lines. From Mother, how to identify Blue Delft china and the chiaroscuro in paintings. From Sister, the importance of political activism and heritage pride. Even from Little Brother, the merits of loyalty and family. She liked to think that her own contributions to the stew were her knack for finding wonder in every cranny, and expressing it for a culture in desperate need of wonder. She had other inheritances too. Ones best not spoken of in the clear light of day. Except in the art she brought.

The Mojave Predicament

Uncle Bill used to take us kids hunting. I can't speak for my siblings, but I always got a knot in my gut from watching the kill moment. The last of those for me was when I raised my .22 rifle and shot off in the distance just as Uncle Bill was homing in on a jackrabbit. I had sabotaged the shot and was banned for life. I didn't exactly mind being banned, as my moral confusion was already confused a-plenty. Because, though I couldn't reconcile the killing act, I enjoyed Aunt Shug's rabbit stew that was always promised afterwards.

The Enthusiast

He loved collecting and visiting famous addresses. The Brady Bunch House was in Studio City, a sleepy little L.A. suburb. The house where the Manson family murders occurred had long been torn down, but the Beverly Hills adjacent location still entertained its ghosts. The stately mansion in Pasadena that had been used for the exterior of Wayne Manor in the 1960s was easily his favorite. His own house was unassuming, sort of like its owner. He'd always dreamt of it being used by Hollywood. Something to give his existence a little legend. Perhaps a juicy crime would have to suffice.

Best Friends

As she rubbed lemongrass oil onto Sophie's delicate fingers to soothe the neuropathy, she couldn't fathom this sentence. She'd always tended to walk between the raindrops, while Sophie had always struggled in life, a dynamic within their long friendship that just subtly but unrelentingly scraped the chalkboard. So, the idea of Sophie being the one to get sick had to offer up a special kind of slap. She wondered if Sophie could appreciate any comeuppance at all to know what lurked defectively within. Imagine being jealous of your friend who has cancer because she's dropped forty-five pounds from the chemo.

Poetry

How you taunted me for years. You knew something I didn't. I tried to play in your sandbox, but never knew the code, and wasn't allowed admission without the secret handshake. We danced a few times in my youth, but I always got antsy with your moves and pulled away toward the loudest guy in the room, he was so damned cool. I saw myself in your mouth once, chomping away at me. I must've been awfully tasty. Today we sort of get each other. Although, I almost think it's better those times when we're just one another's perplexing riddle.

At the End of Lonely Street

He shoves open the rusted door of his RV, drags himself inside, and takes off the wig that's been rendered helmeted by the years-old profusion of Aqua Net, gingerly placing it on the Styrofoam head that sits on his dresser. His knees always require the frozen bag of peas after the gyrating cyclone his legs are lit with every night on stage, as he shakes his Elvis bones for the crowds of Fremont Street. He watches TV until he falls asleep to the mercy of white noise, too damned done to wash the cried-gray torpor of mischance off his neck.

Stripped

On Day 13 of her performance piece, she woke up with pneumonia, and cursed God. She'd waited her whole life to do theatre on the New York stage, and she was finally here. With fair-to-middling reviews, harsh notes from her director each night, and barely the enthusiasm to keep going, why now this? When the performance ended tonight, and she was near collapsing, and the sludge in her chest was unfathomable, and she got the craziest standing ovation ever, her first this run, she could only wonder what mischievous black arts had transpired in the punch-drunk universe of her fever.

Irresistible Collisions

They all lived in the same building, across from the Formosa Café, and were best friends. And for a while, the foursome was on a steady diet of jazz clubs and gay discos. What was hysterical to Stella and June was that Trevelyan and Pierre were huge jazz fans, and the climate among jazz musicians could tend to be somewhat homophobic. The girls got their most satisfying kick out of sitting in a quiet, listening jazz room with the boys, and watching them shout "Work it, Bitch!" after a burning solo by some natty tenor player with a playboy attitude.

Prism

While sitting at a coffeehouse sipping his Americano, he stared at a woman who was pregnant. He found the sight compelling enough for poetry. When she caught him staring, she flipped him off. He'd simply had this overwhelming impulse to pen something beautiful in honor of birth. And she'd had this overwhelming instinct to protect her offspring from the leering predator. As he realized that these confines of perception were simply the way with stories, refracted light at oblique angles, he smiled at the oddity of being the poet in one person's story, while being the villain in someone else's.

Fever Dream

The all-night drugstore may just be that most salacious of all movie tricks. The bottom rung troll the aisles of these bordellos, from drug addicts looking to purchase cheap over-the-counter pills of whatever nature, to young girls loitering the pregnancy test section with nervous constitutions. It courts a permanent midnight, anemic music seeping through speakers like a poisonous gas through the vents, hypnosis the prevalent hue. I dream of floating through this movie, of catching the eye of every downtrodden, of moving inside their pain like a poltergeist, of coursing through their veins like smack, and re-enlivening their dead selves.

Nick the Pig

Nick was from somewhere loud, and he dragged that Loud with him into every bar that featured a girl singer. He loved them. He adored requesting songs, often yelling those requests while they were in the middle of singing. They placated Nick because he tipped well, but a fifty came with a price. He figured they owed him all the requests at his command: Allowing him to sing along, being sympathetic to his loneliness, and tolerating his drunken insults whenever they wouldn't let him misbehave ("you're no Ella!"). Fifty dollars was a small price to pay for a little understanding.

Whiteout

Yellow highlighter. Multicolored sticker tabs. Wite-Out. Time cards. Spreadsheets. Company-wide memos. Downsizing. Rank & file. Customer is always right. Transitioning (PC jargon to soften the blow). Employee of the Year. Everest. Running it up the flagpole. Workforce incentives. Office parties. World's Greatest Boss coffee mug accidentally smashed. Tennis elbow. Sick leave. Sisyphus Complex. Burnout. Was only supposed to be a temp position till the real career kicked in. Forty years later and a gold watch. Adrift in a blizzard of 20 lb. bond, diffuse light, no shadows cast, creating harsh conditions. Working to live, or living to work? Out-of-office autoreply.

Blunted

After about the tenth guy she cheated on her husband with, she stopped counting or remembering. It got too bleak. What she was unloosing, or burying, remained to be known, but she was unstoppable. She did remember #10, perhaps due merely to its decimal nature. He liked bites during sex, and telling jokes (not during sex). He wasn't especially funny, but he did fancy telling people he used to be in Radiohead (he didn't). She found *that* funny. He annoyed her quickly, but she bore the numbing penance, as she imagined her husband at home preparing dinner with their kids.

The Lathers

Stop needing to know what this feeling means. Stop thinking it to death. Stop recoiling from it. It doesn't need to be shushed away. Allow it. You don't need to be talked down from it. Go through it. It exists for a reason. Honor that knot in the gut. It has something to tell you. Don't quarantine it in some kind of self-help bubble that can't allow you to *feel* unless the feeling is a happy one. Own it. Live authentically. Play fiercely. Love messily. Let the lathers we whip ourselves into dissolve into the night, and reform as stars.

The Meeting

Her children weren't here yet, but they promised they'd come. She was nervous to speak tonight; a 30-day chip usually meant you shared. She knew her sharing should be spontaneous and organic, but she'd been a speechwriter in her day, so the spontaneous just wasn't her natural bag. She believed in polish. She was overthinking this. A glance back at the church entrance continued throughout several shares. When she was finally called to receive her 30-day medallion (not her first "30-day" by any stretch), her hands shook as she stood up. The church entrance remained unmerciful of her deepest hopes.

Boundless As the Sea: The Epic Tale of Saucy & Roux

The early morning fog ached Roux's joints, and he craved quiet. Save for the moos of the Guernsey cows, the only other sounds he could bear during the grays were Saucy's meows. Roux loved when Saucy groomed his Shetland fur with her tongue, especially the spot where a fourth leg had never developed. Three-legged Roux, herder to his core, constantly chased the horses, *wobble be damned*, with Saucy exuberantly on his heels. At the end of each glorious day, Saucy kneaded Roux's belly, and when she'd curl into him to sleep, her purrs were all Roux needed in this world.

Sophrosyne

While out walking on a beautiful afternoon, Nate and Maya came across a man pushing his shopping cart laden with critical minutia, who asked for spare change. Nate jumped to the case, responding, "Oh man, I was just gonna ask if YOU had any spare change." The man with the cart, embarrassed, had no retort. "Why?" Maya asked, exasperated by her husband's behavior. Nate gaped at her, annoyed that she didn't get his clever lesson. Oh, Maya got it. Ignoring the man with the lesson, Maya asked the other man's name and shook his hand, honored to make his acquaintance.

Shave

I saw a bearded woman in Starbucks today. I didn't stare. I'm much more evolved than that. And I showed my enlightenment by merely going about my business unfazed. Couldn't get her out of my head though. Inside there—my head, that is—I asked her why she didn't simply get rid of the brazen thing. Just shave. Shave off laughter, finger-pointing. I wanted peace for her. Funny, even in my head she showed me the door, with: Why don't you just shave away the outer layers of your brown skin, shave away discrimination, racial profiling. Cuz that's the answer.

The Sanctification of Eli

Eli had lived in the garden for years, and was never once pooped on by a bird. His neighbor, St. Francis, had been shat upon copiously, which was ironic considering Frank was the patron saint of animals. Even Eli's close friend, the Buddha, had endured his share of pigeon feces. These were the most shamanistic figures in the yard, and he wondered what kind of divine trickster would allow these noble kinsmen to be so soiled, but not him, a mere gnome. When it finally happened, white splats dripping from Eli's red hat, he had to admit, he felt anointed.

AutoCorrect

I shall not soon get over your uninvited proximity into my life, my yearnings to express unencumbered, nay, un-corrected. Let me fall on my own sword, if it be the will of God, for misspelling a word. Those rare times when I have actually needed you, your response, so cold, as if love had never been there, is *"no replacement found."* My tender heart is fragile! Leave me be! Better that than the cruel tease of hope, you swearing allegiance only to steal away in the pitch of night whilst I sleep, left for dead. I might as well be.

The Lovely Juniper

Juniper was lovely. She weighed 450 pounds and had a large patch of hair missing from her scalp due to the alopecia. Third degree burns from the unfortunate house fire pulled at her face and neck. And because of the twisted flesh, her mouth had only just the slightest opening to it any longer, which she thought might help in the weight-loss department, but alas it did not. She was just grateful she lived in a world that didn't judge her for the package she came in. Truly, Juniper was blessed that there was no shallow cruelty in the world.

Vital Signs

He can feel his heartbeat in his hands. They've cuffed them behind him and shoved him into the squad car. He studies the pulse. Slow and hypnotic, maybe 45 bpm. He canvasses the scene before him, as he sits behind the glass, sinking into the rhythm, the architect of this tragedy. They'll wonder how someone could do this. They'll say he has no heart. The pulse moves into his fingertips, as his hands begin the crawl to numbness from the tightness of the handcuffs. He agrees. No one with a heart does this. Tha-thump, tha-thump, tha-thump. Somewhere, life lost meaning.

Knife Sharpening

There wasn't a millisecond in Joy's life when she didn't acutely believe in the hidden cameras. She was burdened by a system of notebooks, red markers, and committees poised to expose and critique her. If she did something stupid, there was a conversation. She told self-effacing jokes to her imagined audience, then laughed at the conceit that this was something she did. It was the amassing of her arsenal against shark bites, the daily sharpening of her knives. When the law of attraction nudged her to change her name to Joy, she truly believed she had a shot at it.

The Ledge

Matt compulsively practiced answers to himself, intended for a boss who was relentless in his criticisms of Matt's work. Matt was so compulsive in rehearsing his defensive dialogue that the neighborhood started to know him as that guy who mumbled to himself. When he got wind of his reputation, and realized how much power he'd given a boss who meant nothing more to him than a paycheck, he felt so chopped off at the knees that he joined a civil servant support group, so that he wouldn't end up as that guy with a gun. Next, Matt bought a gun.

Dance On My Karmic Grave, Why Don't'cha

This morning, an ornate web of glistening trail adorned the entire inside of my car. Who knew that leaving my window cracked open overnight to air out the smell from my surreptitious fast-food binge would allow a snail to infiltrate? How does a slow-inching mollusk get all the way over tire, underside, and frame, to window? Ascending THEN descending? The hours it must've taken to painstakingly rival the palace walls of Versailles. Truly bacchanalian. God's little gift to me for the sin of self-medicating. Wearily add to to-do list: Scrub cabin clean from its magnifying glass onto your flawed life.

Which Ones of Us Are Actually God's Children?

They romp joyfully and seem happy, and I watch them daily through my window. Come winter, I'm afraid they'll find their way in the house, as little rattails can often be seen poking out from an old dropcloth. Soon the traps that've been set will work, and I think about us humans. We spend our entire lives setting up our basic needs and a few creature comforts. And for what? So that at some point a large trap, simply biding its time, snaps us and says, *"It's time to go. You've become too inconvenient for the others who live here."*

She Wouldn't Let Them Win, Even When She Lost

Soft, crisp sunlight dripping off the lacy patterns of breeze-blown curtains. Lemonade feeling like velvet, sliding down a parched throat. Children squealing. Sweet & sour suckers. Double Dutch. Splashes of cool water washing away the fever of the hottest summer the neighborhood had seen. Crips and Bloods seeped out of the cracks like cockroaches when it got this hot. The idyllic world the children knew became hijacked, though they could usually tune the gangs out, in favor of a Velveteen Rabbit euphoria. While Christine and Ruby played hopscotch, Ruby got caught in a crossfire. Her last thought was of lemonade.

Jazz

Once upon a time there was a girl. Otherly in all things. A musician by the compulsion in her gut to assert a unique improvisational voice, and in doing so, unflinchingly state who she was: A woman who was never quite feminine enough. An African-American who was never quite Black enough. An artist who was never quite crafty enough. As inclined as she was to march to her own be-bopping drummer, she also spent an unseemly amount of her life deflecting the throng of pundits that threatened her right to improvise. When all she needed to do, truly... was blow.

Earth

Sometimes he felt overwhelmed by beauty, and his blessed life, and the brilliant humanity of the world. At other times still, he felt of people that they were critically underdeveloped creatures who should kill each other off so that the earth can start fresh. He entertained this latter thought as he dug the hole to bury his crimes, his charred heart. He wondered how deeply he would need to dig, to upturn the damp earth, in order to include himself in the burying, and if forgiveness could be found down there among the earthworms, human bones, and cold, cold dirt.

#1

You say you want to see other women? As long as I'm #1, sure. You say you want a threesome? As long as you, and she, and God know who comes first. You want me to do the chasing? As long as you worship me when I catch you. I'll stuff my better self in a drawer to be in your sphere, which will never disappoint in bleeding me dry of a vibrant lifeforce. It will also not give me your worship, but your contempt. And I will cease being dynamic, vibrant, and alive. But as long as I'm #1...

Canny

He wanted to encounter every single wonder with the patience required to catch every single detail. He wanted to watch a rainfall with the same investment as when he watched a great movie. He wanted to stare at a painting in a museum, and have his life deliriously upended. No, it doesn't move. No, it's not interactive. No, it doesn't trend. There are no platforms. No hashtags. No apps. No followers. No algorithms. It hangs on a wall merely, and blows our illusions to smithereens if we're canny enough to see. He just wanted to be canny enough to see.

So Long Jocko, Goodnight Guts

Her last rebellious act was to steal the blackface lawn jockey from the house across the street. It was 1988, and she'd shared a 2-bedroom condo between five people on Catalina Island. Surely indignant outrage was what made her act. Or was it the claustrophobia? She waited until midnight, borrowed a friend's golf cart, and did the deed. After that, she became safe, common. She often longed for those days when she'd had the audacity to carry plunder across the ocean's breadth on a passenger boat to a San Pedro dumpster in the pitch of night, and call herself righteous.

Good Friday at the Local Mall

It was just another day at his seasonal mall job, but when he saw her approaching, his heart nearly stopped. She held the hand of a little girl whose other tiny hand clung to a father's clutch. A family. They looked so happy. Happier than he had ever been able to make her. Her little girl, who should've been *their* little girl, squealed in delight to be lifted onto the Easter Bunny's lap for a photo. It was of little comfort to the unseen man inside the costume that no one could sense the heartbreak inside that giant smiling head.

Those Who Read Books

Those who read books travel the world and time itself. Are explorers, adventurers, discoverers. Take on beggars and kings with no thought in the ranking. Have their minds forced open and their spirits ever expanding in insatiable hunger for more. Those who read books fill themselves with wonder. Know that a book is a friend, a teacher, a priest, an agitator. Are not afraid to be made uncomfortable. Grow the wings that continue, muscle by muscle, to sprout upon reaching "The End" time and time anew. Fly. Fall. Fly again. Those who read books are changed. And glad of it.

Corner of Hollywood & Hell

Last night around 3am, I stood in line behind a seedy Marilyn Monroe and Sammy Davis Jr. at the 7-Eleven, ingesting the washed green mesmer of those witching hours. The cashier, already glazed over with the ennui of midnight, rolled his eyes as the duo paid for their liquor and cigarettes and never dropped character. The cashier just saw crazy, but I gave them an audience, asking Marilyn how it felt singing Happy Birthday for the president. Sammy laughed in that stomped-footed way he was known for. The cashier surely placed our trio on Fruitcake Avenue. Oh, dearie. Just leap.

Angela Carole Brown is the recipient of the North Street Book Prize in literary fiction for her novel *Trading Fours*, and the SoulWord Magazine Poetry Prize for her poem "Cotton Candy." She is also the author of the novel *The Assassination of Gabriel Champion*, the memoir *The Kidney Journals: Memoirs of a Desperate Lifesaver*, and the poetry collections *Bones* and *Viscera*. She writes the blog Bindi Girl Chronicles. She has also been on the L.A. music scene for over three decades as a singer, songwriter, and recording artist, has produced several albums of music in the genres of jazz and folk, and is the lead singer in Elvis Schoenberg's Orchestre Surreal. She is featured in the documentary film *The Goddess Project*. *Aleatory on the Radio* marks her first short story collection.

www.angelacarolebrown.com
www.bit.ly/BooksByAngelaCaroleBrown
Facebook @angelacarolebrown
Instagram @bindigirlchronicles
Twitter @angelacarolebro

www.ingramcontent.com/pod-product-compliance
Lightning Source LLC
Chambersburg PA
CBHW050737250626
47155CB00005B/1808